jE   Smith
        Glasses.   c.2

GLASSES

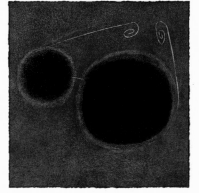

WHO NEEDS 'EM?

BY LANE SMITH

VIKING

To
Salvino d'Armato,
Ben Franklin,
and
Saint Jerome

—L.S.

VIKING
Published by the Penguin Group
Viking Penguin, A division of Penguin Books USA Inc.,
375 Hudson Street, New York, New York 10014, U.S.A.
Penguin Books Ltd, 27 Wrights Lane, London W8 5TZ, England
Penguin Books Australia LTD, Ringwood, Victoria, Australia
Penguin Books Canada Ltd, 2801 John Street, Markham, Ontario, Canada L3R 1B4
Penguin Books (N.Z.) Ltd, 182–190 Wairau Road, Auckland 10, New Zealand
Penguin Books Ltd, Registered Offices: Harmondsworth, Middlesex, England
First published in 1991 by Viking Penguin, a division of Penguin Books USA Inc.

1 2 3 4 5 6 7 8 9 10
Copyright © Lane Smith, 1991 All rights reserved
Library of Congress Cataloging in Publication Data
Smith, Lane. Glasses (who needs 'em?) / by Lane Smith   p.   cm.
Summary: A boy is unhappy about having to wear glasses, until his doctor
provides an imaginative list of well-adjusted eyeglass wearers.
[1. Eyeglasses—Fiction.] I. Title. PZ7.S6538Ev 1991 [E]—dc20
ISBN 0-670-84160-9 91-9827 CIP AC

Printed in U.S.A. Set in Stone Sans
The illustrations are rendered in oil on board

Design: Molly Leach, New York, New York

I told him,
"No way."

He said, "Young man, if
you are worried about
looking a little different..."

I said, "I'm worried
about looking like a dork."

He said, "Lots of folks wear
glasses and love 'em."

He said...

"Your mom wears glasses...

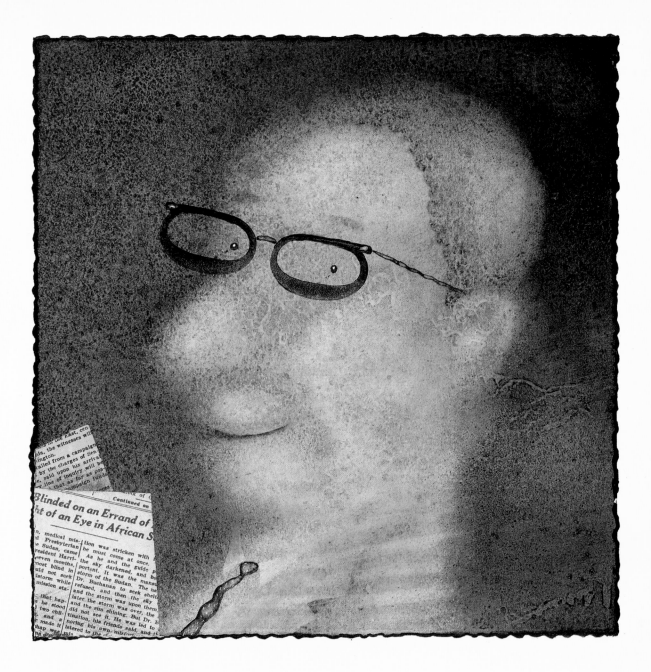

...your dad wears glasses...

...your sister wears glasses..."

"My sister," I said,
"wears green rubber bands
in her hair and T-shirts
with unicorns on 'em."

"Okay then," he said.
"What about famous inventors...

...or 'monster-movie' stuntpeople, hmmm?

Why even *entire planets* wear glasses!"

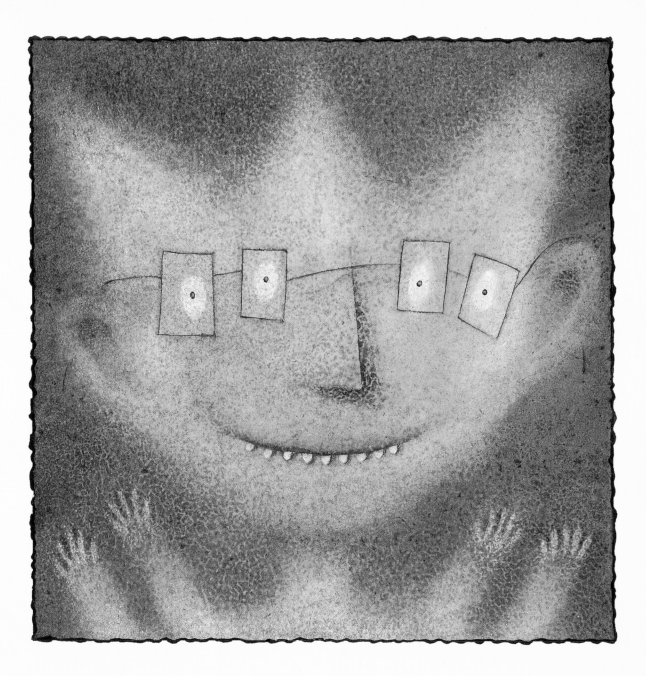

I thought my doctor might be exaggerating
just a little with that last "planets" statement.
I asked, "Do little green men wear glasses?

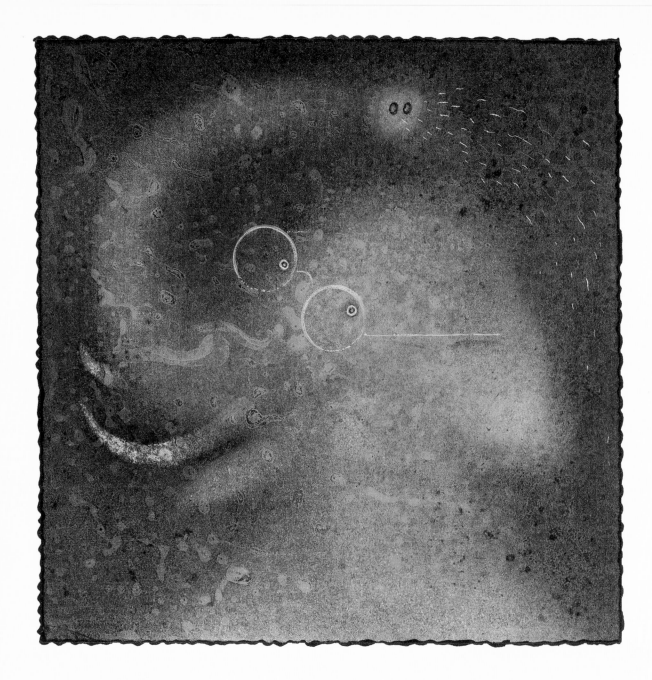

Do pink elephants?

Do Hong-Kong-Flu bugs?"

YES!
YES!
YES!

was his answer
(I thought it might be).
He continued...

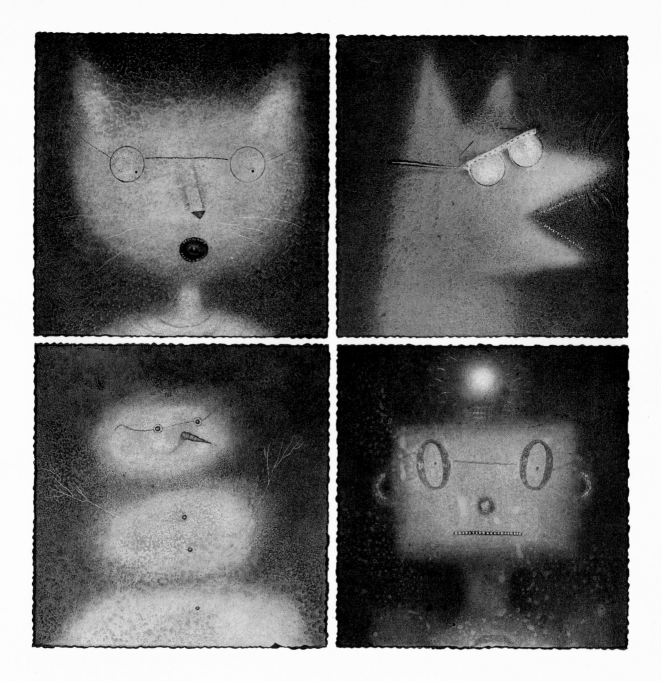

"...But you left out cats and dogs and
snowmen and robots!" He was very excited.
I was going to suggest maybe he was
putting too much sugar on his cereal...

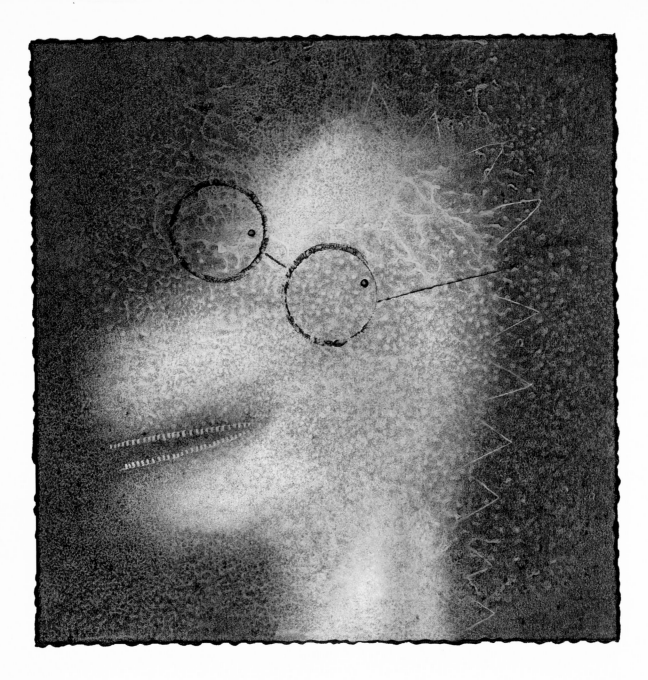

...but he started up again.
"Giant dinosaurs wear glasses...

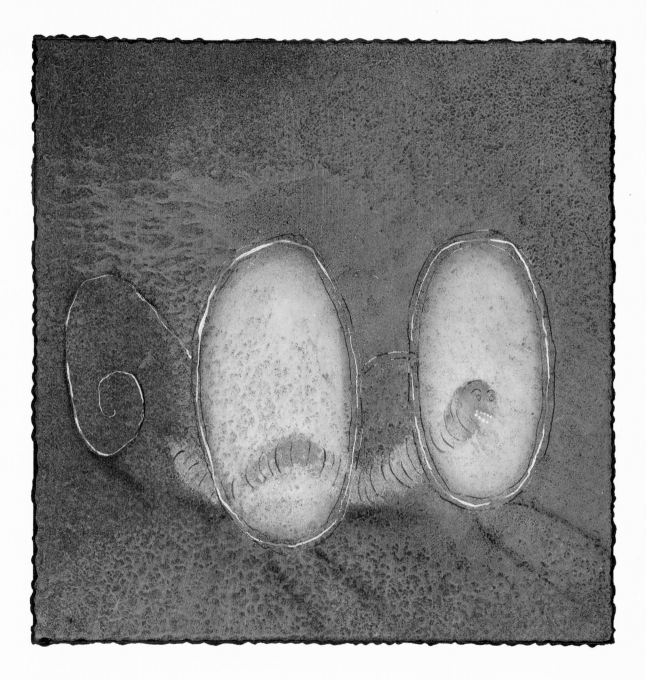

...and little worms...

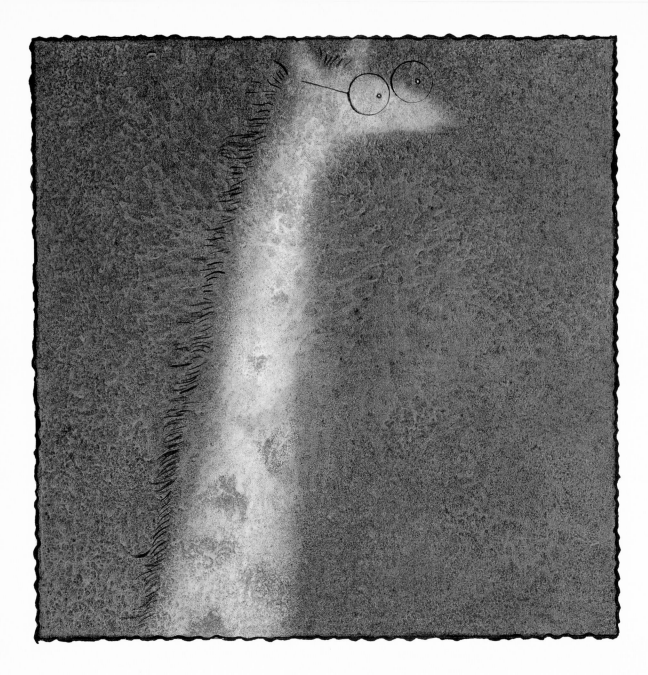

...and tall giraffes...

...and short fuzzy bunnies."

"Well, if you're going to insist on rabbits wearing glasses, maybe we should give some specs to their carrots too!"

"Don't be ridiculous," he answered. "Carrots don't *need* glasses...

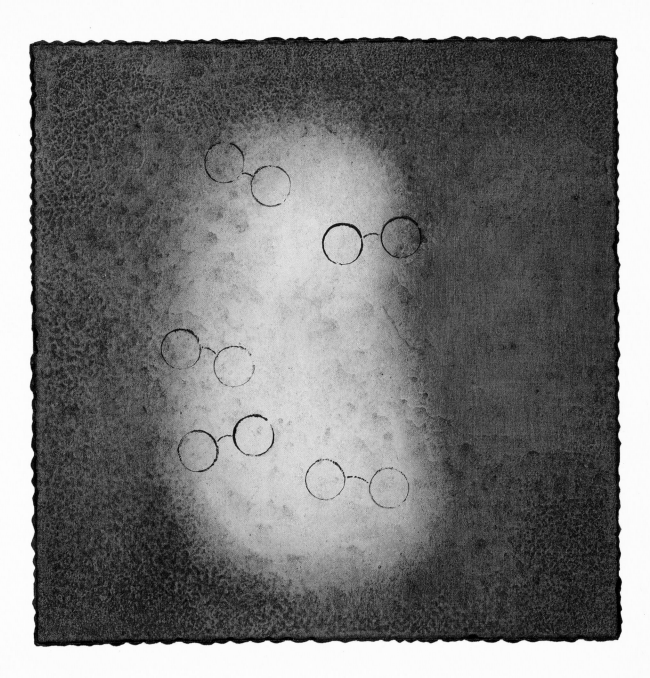

...potatoes however..."

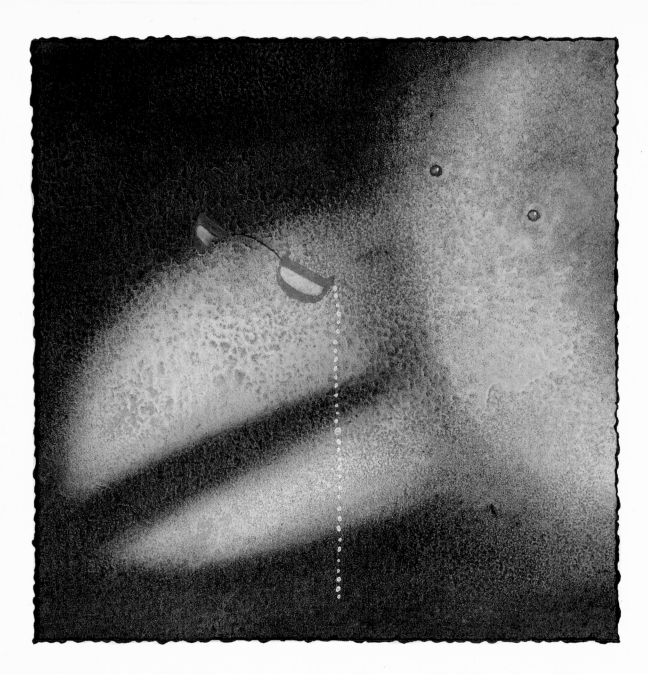

"Oh brother, now I understand...
you're a loony aren't you?
I bet you see glasses on cuckoo birds...

...and buffoonish baboons..."

"Now you're catching on...
allow me then to also
point out sheep and opossum
and chameleon and fish

and oil painting

and sock puppet

and chameleon

and crocodile

and chameleon...

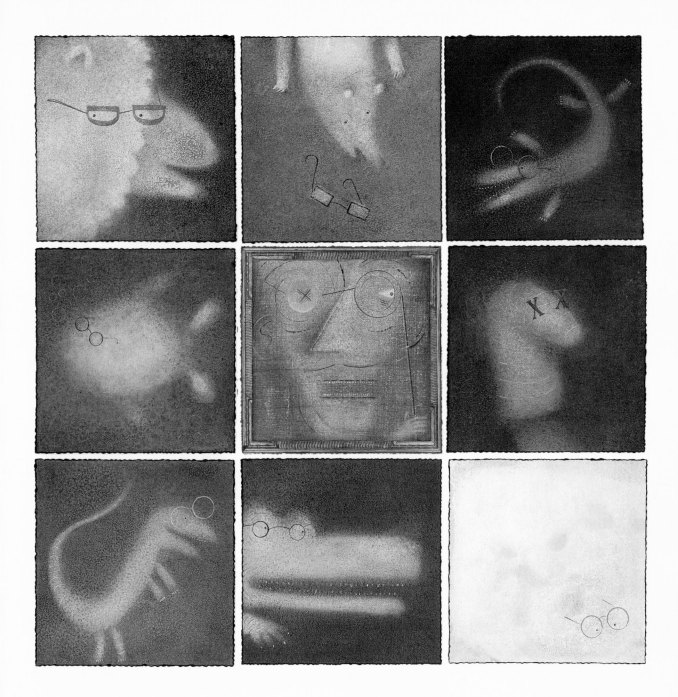

They all wear glasses! Oh, and...ahem...

...I do too!"

"You need them," I said.
"You've been seeing things!"
And with that, I started to leave.

"Just a minute, young man...

I told him, "The gold-wire rims will be just fine."